This book belongs to

....

This is the story of a room full of straw,

A strange little man and a magic trapdoor.

You can read it in bed, in a chair, on the floor!

There's something else. Can you guess what?

On every page there's a cotton reel to spot.

Rumpelstiltskin

Nick and Claire Page

Illustrations by Sara Baker

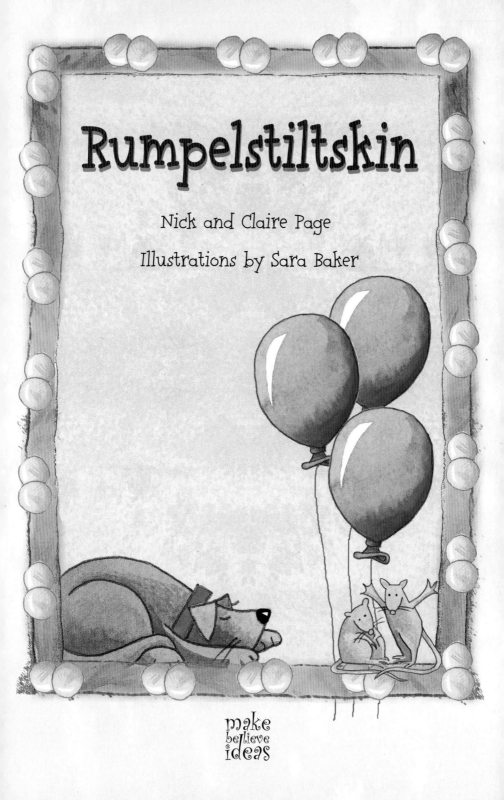

make
believe
ideas

There once was a miller, who lied to the king,
"I have a sweet daughter called Geraldine.
She turns yellow straw into gold with one spin!"

The king locked the girl in a room full of straw,
Saying, "Spin me gold or you'll die, for sure."
Geraldine wept. Then guess what she saw!

From a door in the floor a little man sprang,
"Spin straw into gold? Why, do it I can!"
"Give me your necklace and I am your man!"

Geraldine promised. And so he sang:
"Yellow straw, threads of gold!
Spinning magic now behold!"
And the straw turned to gold.
Then he left through the door
in the floor.

The king was delighted with his golden thread.
"Now spin this lot too," he greedily said.
"In time for tomorrow or off with your head!"

The miller's girl cried when she saw more straw,
Then out came the man from his magic trapdoor:
"Give me your ring and I'll help you once more."

Geraldine promised. And so he sang:
"Yellow straw, threads of gold!
Spinning magic now behold!"

And the straw turned to gold.
Then he left through the door
in the floor.

The king gave her more straw.
"Here, have one last try!"
Then went off again, as the girl gave a sigh,
"I have nothing to pay with. I'll have to die!"

13

When the little man saw the straw in a pile,
He gave her a look, both cunning and wild.
"Do it, I will, but I'll have your first child!"

Sadly, Geraldine promised.
And so he sang:
"Yellow straw, threads of gold!
Spinning magic now behold!"
And the straw turned to gold.
Then he left through the door
in the floor.

The girl married the king, had a baby next year,
And she'd almost forgotten the feeling of fear,
When from his trapdoor, the man reappeared.

"I've come for that baby, asleep in the bed!"
"Not Gerald!" cried Geraldine. "Take me instead!"
"I'll set you a test," the little man said.

"For three days at sunset, I'll visit again,
And give you three chances to guess
my real name.
Get it wrong and the baby is mine all the same."
**And he left through the door
in the floor.**

The queen sent servants to find out his name,
But they had no answer when he came again.
"Is it Caspar?" she asked. "Or Bert? Or Elaine?"

"WRONG!" said the little man.
And he left through the door
in the floor.

Next day was no better and when he arrived,
The queen couldn't guess it, hard though she tried!
"Leonardo?" she asked. "Or Jones? Or McBride?"

"WRONG AGAIN!" said the little man.
And he left through the door
in the floor.

By now the queen thought her hopes were all shot,
But then came a messenger, sweaty and hot.
"My Lady!" he cried. "We've hit the jackpot!"

"In a house by the mountains, I saw a wee man,
Shouting with glee at his wild, cunning plan.
Singing, 'Guess, she will not. Rumpelstiltskin I am!'

That evening as Geraldine poured out some wine,
The little gold spinner appeared, right on time.
"Last chance!" he said. "Then the boy will be mine!
Or if it's too difficult, then just give in."

"Not so fast," said the queen.
"Let the wheel have a spin.
Is it Boris?
Or Britney?
Or RUMPELSTILTSKIN!"

Rumpelstiltskin cried, "Noooooooo!"
Then he bounced round the room,
He swelled like a toad and his head turned maroon.
And BANG! Rumpelstiltskin burst like a balloon!

Now the point of this story, we must say to you,
Is: Don't ever lie about things you can't do.
Don't be greedy for gold, even if you're a king,
And never trust someone called...
RUMPELSTILTSKIN!

Ready to tell

Oh no! Some of the pictures from this story have been mixed up! Can you retell the story and point to each picture in the correct order?

Picture dictionary

Encourage your child to read these harder words from the story and gradually develop their basic vocabulary.

baby   castle   girl

king   miller   mountains

queen   spinning wheel   straw

Key words

Here are some key words used in context.
Help your child to use other words from
the border in simple sentences.

"What **can** I do?" she cried.

There **was** a door in the floor.

"I can spin gold," he **said**.

The servant rode **away**.

"**No**," said the queen.

Make a name-spinner

Rumpelstiltskin was a spinning ace, but could he have spun your name onto a heart? It's easier than you might think!

You will need

some strong cardboard • an old CD or round plastic lid • a pencil, and crayons or colouring pens • scissors • two pieces of string, each about 40cm long

What to do

1 Lay the CD or plastic lid on the cardboard. Draw around this and cut out the circle to make a disc.

2 Draw a faint pencil line across the disc's diameter. Mark a point on this line, about 1cm in from the edge. Ask a grown-up to make a hole through the card at both points.

3 Draw a big, colourful heart on one side of the card.

4 Turn the card over and write your name on this side.

5 Knot the ends of one length of string together to make a loop. Thread the loop through one hole in the circle and then thread the knotted end through the loop. Pull the knotted end until the string is taut. Repeat, using the other length of string and the other hole.

6 Holding a string loop in each hand, twist the disc until the string is wound tight. Quickly pull the strings apart and the disc will spin like a wheel. Watch while it spins and you should see your name inside the heart!